The Junior Novelization

ISBN: 978-0-7364-2960-3

randomhouse.com/kids

Printed in the United States of America

10 9 8 7 6 5 4 3 2 1

Disney
WRECK-IT RALPH

The Junior Novelization

Adapted by Irene Trimble

Random House 🏠 New York

Prologue

Welcome to Litwak's Family Fun Center

For more than thirty years, Litwak's Family Fun Center had been entertaining children. Two generations of kids knew that if you wanted to play the best video games, Litwak's was *the* place to go.

The atmosphere in the arcade was one of ringing bells and electronic beeps. Kids raced between rows of fighting, dancing, racing, and first-person-shooter game consoles, testing their skills against various video characters.

The arcade even had a few original 8-bit games from way back in the 1980s. The characters in those games were pixilated and looked more like clumps of little colored dots than the movie-like realism found in modern games, but they were *classics*!

One of those original games was called *Fix-It Felix Jr.* The game's official Good Guy was a little fellow named Fix-It Felix, outfitted with work gloves, a tool belt, and a gleaming gold magic hammer.

But Felix wasn't the most exciting character in the game. That honor belonged to the game's Bad Guy, Wreck-It Ralph.

Whenever a kid put a coin into the game console, Ralph leaped on-screen with huge fists, torn overalls, and a furious attitude, yelling, "I'M GONNA WRECK IT!"

As each game started, Ralph climbed up the side of a pixilated apartment building in a place called Niceland and smashed the structure to pieces. Bricks rained down while frightened Nicelanders peered out from the windows.

"FIX IT, FELIX!" the Nicelanders would shout.

Then Felix would show up, cheerful and calm, holding his magic hammer. If a player handled the joystick skillfully enough, Felix would follow Ralph up the side of the apartment building, fixing all the broken windows and loose bricks.

Once Felix fixed the entire building and reached the roof, the player won! On the screen, the Nicelanders cheered as they presented Felix with a shiny gold medal.

But what about Ralph, the Bad Guy? Game after game, the Nicelanders hoisted him up and tossed him off the roof. He always landed facedown in the mud at the bottom of the building.

For kids, there was something simple and fun about the story of Ralph and Felix. That's why the game was still popular after many years, despite its old-fashioned style.

In fact, every video game in Litwak's arcade told a story. But the stories weren't exactly what Mr. Litwak and the kids thought they were. Every night, when the video arcade closed . . . the real action started.

CHAPTER

1

Ralph sat on a little folding chair and looked at the dozen or so other Bad Guys sitting in a circle around the room.

"My name's Wreck-It Ralph," he began. "I'm nine feet tall. I weigh 643 pounds. I can't walk down the street without causing major structural damage to buildings." He shrugged. "I guess that kind of makes me the Bad Guy."

"Hi, Ralph," the group answered in unison.

Ralph nodded as his gaze fell on the banner pinned up over the snack table that read BAD-ANON: ONE GAME AT A TIME. Leaving his game and traveling through the power cord to attend a support group for Bad Guys had seemed like a good idea earlier in the evening. But now Ralph wondered whether anyone could truly understand how he felt.

"Look," Ralph said, "I'm great at what I do; I'm probably the best I know. But the problem is that fixing stuff is the object of the game. Fix-It Felix Jr.—he's the Good Guy. You know, he's nice enough as Good Guys go; definitely fixes stuff really well. But if you've got a *magic hammer* . . . how hard can it be?"

Ralph paused, thinking how easily Felix swung his little hammer and magically fixed whatever Ralph had wrecked. Ralph had the hard job! He had to tear apart the Nicelanders' building and smash bricks with his *bare hands*. Felix just showed up and cried, "I CAN FIX IT!" From there, with a little help from a game player, everything practically repaired itself.

Ralph sighed. "And when Felix does a good job, *he* gets a medal. But are there medals for the sweet science of wrecking? To that I say, *'Ha!'* And . . . *no,* there aren't."

It was true. In all the years that Ralph had been wrecking the Nicelanders' building, they had never given him a reward of any kind. Instead, they shrieked in terror whenever they saw him coming. And, of course, there was that big mud puddle.

"Thirty years I've been doing this. I've seen a lot of other games come and go. Kind of sad," Ralph said, reflecting. "Look, a steady arcade gig is nothing to sneeze at. I'm very lucky. But if you've been doing this as long as I have, it starts to feel hard to love your job when no one else seems to like you for doing it."

Ralph paused again. If only the Nicelanders would acknowledge his value in the game. Even something simple like a pie would be nice. A medal would be even better. Felix always received a lot of pies and medals.

"Every day after work, Felix and the Nicelanders go hang out in their apartments, which Felix has just fixed," Ralph continued. "They go to their homes, and I go to mine, which happens to be a pile of garbage in the dump. You might call it a lonely cesspit of despair on the outskirts of humanity. I call it home. That's where I live. That's where I go.

"I guess I can't bellyache too much. I've got my bricks. I've got my stump. It looks uncomfortable, but it's actually fine. I'm . . . I'm good."

Ralph closed his eyes for a moment. "But if I'm really honest with myself, I see Felix up there, getting patted on the back, people giving him pie and thanking him and so happy to see him all the time. Sometimes I think, *Man, it must be nice being the Good Guy.*"

CHAPTER

2

"**N**ice share," the Bad-Anon leader said as Ralph finished his story. "As fellow Bad Guys, we've all felt what you're feeling. And we've come to terms with it."

Ralph glanced around the room at the other video game Bad Guys. There was Zombie, whose clothes (and skin) always seemed to be falling off . . . Cyborg, part man and part machine . . . Satine, with red skin, a purple cape, and horns . . . and all kinds of other characters, big, small, scary, and not-so-scary. Every single one of them was nodding sympathetically.

"Really?" Ralph asked.

A huge, barrel-chested Russian wrestler raised his hand. "I am Bad Guy," he announced in a heavy accent. "I relate to you, Ralph." He shrugged. "I say to myself, 'You are Bad Guy. But that does not mean you are *bad guy*.'"

Everyone in the room applauded.

"Right," Ralph mumbled uncertainly. "But, uh, you lost me there."

Zombie tried to explain. "Labels not make you happy—'good,' 'bad'—you must love *you*," he groaned.

"Yeah, inside *here*," Cyborg agreed as he reached into Zombie's chest and ripped out his heart.

"Whoa!" Ralph shouted a little too loudly, cringing at the sight of a dripping heart. Zombie wasn't hurt, of course. He just happened to be the sort of Bad Guy character whose heart could be ripped out. But Ralph found the whole display a little unsettling.

The Bad-Anon leader attempted to refocus the discussion. "Question, Ralph: we've been asking you to Bad-Anon for years now, and tonight you finally show up. Why is that?"

"I dunno," Ralph said, staring at the floor. "I just felt like coming. I suppose it has something to do with the fact that, well, today is the thirtieth anniversary of my game."

"Happy anniversary, Ralph!" Satine exclaimed.

"Thanks, Satine," Ralph replied with a nod. "But it's no big deal."

"No, Ralph—thirty years?" the Bad-Anon leader said, sounding a little surprised. "Not many games can claim that."

Zombie growled, "Zombie so jealous!"

"Jealous? Of what?" Ralph asked. "It's not like I've got anything to show for it."

The Russian wrestler disagreed. "Ralph, this not true. You, my friend, are really good Bad Guy!"

"But here's the thing," Ralph said. "I don't want to be the Bad Guy anymore."

Every Bad Guy in the room gasped. "Good heavens!" Satine exclaimed.

"You can't mess with the program, Ralph!" Cyborg warned. "You're not *going Turbo,* are you?"

"*Turbo?* No, I'm not *going Turbo,*" Ralph replied hastily. Even he knew that some kinds of behavior would never be acceptable. And going Turbo . . . well, that was one of them. Chaos and disaster were sure to follow. But was the situation really *that* serious?

"Come on, guys," Ralph continued. "Is it *Turbo* to want something better for your life?"

"Yes!" everyone replied together.

"Ralph," the group leader said in a soothing tone, "we can't change who we are, and the sooner we accept that, the better off your game and your life will be. Now let's close out with the Bad Guy Affirmation."

Together the group stood up, shut their eyes, and held

hands. "I am Bad," they recited in unison. "And that's good. I will never be Good. And that's not bad. There's no one I'd rather be than me."

Ralph, however, stood with his eyes open and his mouth closed. He didn't believe a word of it.

CHAPTER

3

As the Bad-Anon meeting broke up, the leader called out, "Okay, gang, see you next Thursday."

"Hang in there," Satine said, giving Ralph a supportive pat on the back. Ralph nodded and left.

As he headed toward the game's exit, Ralph grabbed a few snacks. The game where Bad-Anon meetings were held always had plenty of fruit, and Ralph didn't want to waste it.

Then Ralph hurried to join the other Bad Guys on a small train that carried them into a tunnel. The train zipped through the game's electrical cord, finally stopping at Game Central Station. This was the power hub of the video arcade. Every game was plugged into Game Central, and it was a stopover for anyone traveling from one game to another.

Everyone hopped off the train and headed up another

tunnel that led into Game Central's soaring interior. As Ralph passed into the station, a buzzer sounded.

Surge Protector, a stiff-looking fellow in full uniform, stepped up to Ralph. "Random security check, sir," he said.

Ralph grimaced. "You always stop me."

"I'm just a Surge Protector doing his job, sir. Name?"

"You know my name," Ralph grumbled.

"NAME?" Surge Protector demanded.

"Wreck-It Ralph." Ralph rolled his eyes.

"Did you bring any fruit with you?"

Ralph quickly hid the fruit treats behind his back.

Surge Protector continued. "Where are you headed?"

Ralph sighed. *Fix-It Felix Jr.*"

"Anything to declare?" Surge Protector asked.

"Yes," Ralph muttered. "I hate you."

"I get that a lot," Surge Protector replied, with no expression. "Proceed."

Ralph walked into the crowd, pulling out the hidden fruit once he was out of Surge Protector's sight. Other game characters gave him a wide berth. Ralph could hear their whispers. "That's Wreck-It Ralph. Bad Guy. Better get out of his way."

As Ralph continued through the station, he passed several public-service signs—reminders to be careful when traveling between games. Everyone enjoyed being able to visit friends or sightsee when off-duty, but there were dangers.

The big thing to remember was that you could only regenerate in your own game. If you had an accident or were defeated by someone else while inside another game, that was the end. There was no "bouncing back."

Ralph sighed as he passed a group of homeless characters clustered against a wall. They had been forced to abandon their games long before. Most had fled broken game consoles on the verge of being unplugged. They'd had no choice! If they'd stayed when the games' electrical cords were pulled, they'd have been destroyed along with the game consoles themselves.

Ralph looked down at a cute little orange character. The poor guy held a sign that read GAME UNPLUGGED: PLEASE HELP!

Ralph offered him the fruit and smiled warmly. "Hang in there, dude."

Finally, Ralph reached the *Fix-It Felix Jr.* portal. Suddenly, a buzzer sounded. Ralph rolled his eyes as Surge Protector appeared . . . *again.*

"Name?" he said to Ralph. This guy clearly needed more memory.

From there, Ralph jumped onto a small train that carried him through the electrical cord back to *Fix-It Felix Jr.* After stepping into his own game, Ralph headed for his pile of bricks. Then he stopped short.

He heard the very loud and distinct sounds of party horns and music. Ralph gazed upward at the penthouse of the Nicelander building. It was a huge party, in full swing!

"I am Bad. And that's good," Ralph told himself, hoping the affirmation would make him feel better. "There's no one I'd rather be than me."

But the affirmation didn't seem to help. Ralph plunked down onto his stump and sighed.

A crack and a sizzle overhead forced him to look up. WE LOVE YOU, FELIX! blazed across the sky in colorful fireworks.

"Ah, great," Ralph muttered.

He grabbed two empty bottles from the junk heap and held them up to his eyes as binoculars. Now he could see into the top apartment, where Felix and the Nicelanders were dancing and laughing. A huge buffet was set out for everyone to enjoy—everyone except Ralph.

"Happy thirtieth anniversary?" Ralph exclaimed, spotting a colorful sign. "They're having a party without me?"

Determined, Ralph stood up and began walking toward the building. This was an event that everyone in the game deserved to celebrate—including the Bad Guy!

CHAPTER

4

As he approached the penthouse door, Ralph could hear the guests chatting happily inside.

"Great party, Felix!" Nicelander Roy was saying.

"Why, thank you, Roy," Felix replied.

Out in the hallway, Ralph pressed his giant finger to the tiny doorbell.

"I'll get it, Felix," he heard Nicelander Gene say. A moment later, Gene opened the door, took one look at Ralph—and slammed the door shut.

"It's Ralph!" Gene whimpered.

"Ralph who?" another Nicelander asked.

"Wreck-It Ralph!" Gene squealed.

"Hide the finery!" someone shouted.

Unfortunately, Ralph heard the entire conversation as he waited, still outside the door.

"Felix, fix it!" Nicelander Roy pleaded.

"Oh, of course. I'll go talk to him. Carry on, everyone," Felix replied. Ralph heard his footsteps approaching the door.

Then Felix slipped into the hallway, closing the door behind him. "Ralph, can I help you?" he asked politely.

Ralph shuffled his big feet and said, "Hey, Felix. I just wanted to check on you. I saw a big explosion or something over the building. Is everything okay?"

Felix smiled. "Oh, those were just fireworks."

"Ohhhh. Fireworks," Ralph said. "Okay, whew. You had me scared there. Is it, uh, somebody's birthday?"

"Well . . . ," Felix said reluctantly, "it's *kind of* a birthday. More of an anniversary. The thirtieth anniversary of our game, actually."

"Is that tonight?!" Ralph said, hoping to sound surprised. "I'm such a dummy with things. Yup, we've had a heck of a run, haven't we? Every one of us doing our part for this game. Anyway, congratulations."

"Thank you," Felix said politely. "And you, too."

A turtle poked his head out the door. Ralph's jaw dropped. That turtle was not even a *Fix-It Felix Jr.* character! Felix and the Nicelanders had invited someone from another game, but they had ignored Ralph.

"Just a heads-up, Felix," the turtle said, "they're

bringing the cake out in a few shakes." The turtle turned and slammed the door again.

"Cake?" Ralph asked. "Never had it. No one ever seems to throw it out, so it never ends up in the dump. So I've never actually tasted it."

Felix looked uncomfortable. Finally, he said, "I don't suppose you'd like to come in and have a slice, would you?"

Ralph grinned from ear to ear and pushed past Felix.

"Don't mind if I do," Ralph said, striding through the door, ripping it off its hinges. As he straightened up, Ralph's head crashed through the ceiling. A big chunk of plaster fell out...and dropped on Felix, who flickered and fell to the floor. A little flower floated just above his motionless body.

The room went silent as the Nicelanders stared in horror.

After a long moment, Felix flickered again, this time regenerating back into existence. "I'm okay! Fit as a fiddle!" he called, popping to his feet. "You know Ralph."

Ralph forced a smile as he looked at the cringing guests. He stooped and greeted each one. "Evening, Nel. Lucy. Don. Dana."

"Deanna," said Deanna coldly.

Then Ralph turned to Nicelander Gene, a character he often tossed across the screen during official game play.

"Big Gene," Ralph said, nodding amiably.

"Why is *he* here?" Gene snapped, clearly irritated.

"He's just here for a slice of cake," Felix explained.

Ralph shrugged as he looked at their hostile faces. "And . . . I am a big part of this game, technically speaking." He bent down to Gene's level. "Why are *you* here, Gene?"

"Oh, look! The cake!" Felix announced nervously as Nicelander Mary wheeled in an elaborate cake that looked just like the Niceland apartments.

CHAPTER
5

The anniversary cake was impressive. It was tall and frosted, with candy windows and sugar that had been spun on top to create a sweet version of the "We Love You, Felix!" fireworks.

"Well, I'll be dipped, Mary," Felix said happily. "You've really outdone yourself."

The Nicelanders gathered around the cake. "Nice work with the fondant!" Roy exclaimed.

"And look! There's all of us at the top," Gene said, pointing.

"Oh, we're just adorable," someone else said. All the Nicelanders were pleased.

Mary, dressed in a prim little purple suit, smiled. "And each apartment is everyone's favorite flavor," she said proudly. "Norwood's is red velvet."

"Guilty!" Nicelander Norwood laughed.

"And lemon for Lucy. Rum cake for Gene. And for Felix—"

"Vanilla!" the Nicelanders shouted in unison.

Ralph stood behind everyone and looked at the cake. A little candy Felix stood on the roof, smiling and reaching for a medal. At the bottom of the building, in the mud, sat an ugly, pitiful candy Ralph.

"And this mud where I'm stuck—what is it made of?" Ralph asked.

"Chocolate," Mary replied.

"Never been real fond of chocolate," Ralph said.

"Well, I did not know that," Mary responded.

Then he nodded at the little Ralph figurine. "One other little thing. I hate to be picky, but do you really think this looks like me?" He bent down and put his face next to the figurine for comparison.

"Yes," Mary said simply.

"Artistic interpretation," Felix said helpfully.

"Well, in my interpretation, this little guy would be a lot happier if you put him on top with everyone else," Ralph replied, reaching out toward the candy Ralph. To everyone's shock, he picked up the figurine and placed it on top of the cake, smearing Mary's frosting.

"No, no, no!" Gene said quickly. "There's no room for

you up there." He knocked the candy Ralph back down into the mud, messing up the cake even further.

"Well, what about this?" Ralph said, taking the miniature Felix from the top of the cake and moving him into the mud. "We can make some room. There, that's much better."

The Nicelanders gasped in horror. "How about we just eat the cake?" Felix said anxiously.

"Hang on," Gene said. "Felix needs to be on the roof, because everyone is cheering for him and he's about to get his medal."

Ralph reached in again and took the medal off the cake, breaking the spun-sugar fireworks. "Then how about we just take that medal and give it to little Ralph for a change?"

The crowd stared wide-eyed as Ralph put the medal on little Ralph.

"Now you're just being ridiculous," Roy said irritably. "Only Good Guys win medals, and you, sir, are no Good Guy."

Ralph stared at them all. "Well, suppose I *could* win a medal! Then you'd let me up here, right?"

"Ralph," Gene said with a mocking smile, "if you win a medal, we'll let you *live* up here in the penthouse." The

Nicelanders all laughed, and Gene pulled the medal off the little candy Ralph and put it on the candy Felix. "But it will never happen, because you're just the Bad Guy who wrecks the building."

"No, I'm not!" Ralph said a little too loudly.

"Yes, you are!" Gene dropped the little candy Ralph in the mud, upside down.

Frustrated, Ralph raised his huge fists. Then he slammed them down on the cake, splattering it everywhere. "No, I'm NOT!" he shouted.

Everyone froze. Ralph looked around at the Nicelanders' distraught faces, now covered in cake. He dropped his head.

"You know what?" Ralph said. "I'm going to go win a medal. The shiniest medal this place has ever seen!" Then he turned toward the door. "Good night. Thank you for the party."

Roy turned to the other Nicelanders. "Is he being serious?"

"Please," scoffed Gene. "Where is a Bad Guy going to get a medal?"

CHAPTER

6

Miserable, Ralph headed out through the tunnel to Game Central Station. From there he entered another game, where he knew there was a small, quiet restaurant.

He walked into the dining room and sat alone, sipping a soda. The place was filled with Good Guys. Ralph noticed they all had medals or trophies. And they all wore smiles indicating that they had come out on top again.

"Now, come on," he told his server. "Where can a guy like me go and win a medal?"

"I don't know what to tell you," the server said. "Maybe someone left a medal here. You're welcome to look through the Lost and Found."

So Ralph pulled out the old Lost and Found box from a closet down the hall. As he dug through it, a large, fully armored soldier walked by and bumped into him.

"Hey!" Ralph objected.

The soldier didn't reply. He seemed dazed and kept trying to walk into the wall, as if he should be able to go right through it. He kept muttering, "We are humanity's last hope. Destroy all cy-bugs. . . ."

"Uh, are you okay there?" Ralph asked, gently tapping the soldier's shoulder.

The fellow whirled around. His eyes were wide open as he practically shrieked in Ralph's face, "We've only been plugged in a week! And every day it's 'climb the building,' and then 'fight the bugs'!"

He grabbed Ralph desperately.

"Hey! Easy on the overalls, spaceman," Ralph said, holding his palms out to keep a safe distance from the crazed soldier. "It's tough everywhere, all right?"

Ralph turned and started to walk away.

"And all for what?" the soldier squealed. "A lousy medal!"

Ralph stopped.

"Medal?" Turning around to face the soldier, he said, "You win a medal?"

"Yeah!" the soldier replied. "The Medal of Heroes!"

Ralph considered. "Is it shiny?"

"Uh, pretty shiny," the soldier said.

"And it says HERO on it, and you win it by climbing a

building?" Ralph continued with increasing excitement.

"And fighting bugs!" the soldier screamed.

Ralph approached the soldier carefully. "Is there any way I could go with you to your game and maybe get one of those medals?"

"Negatory!"

"Does that mean maybe?"

"No!" the soldier barked. "Look, only the bravest and the best serve in our corps—"

Just then, a tiny bug hopped onto Ralph's shoulder.

The soldier shrieked in terror. *"Ahh-hoo-hoo!"* Then he turned and ran straight into the wall, knocking himself out cold.

Ralph stared at the soldier. Then he looked at his armor. The battle gear covered the soldier's entire body, from head to toe.

Several minutes later, the soldier exited the restaurant. But he looked different. He seemed a little too large for his outfit. His head completely filled his helmet, and there were little fringes of brown hair at the edges of his face.

The "soldier" lifted one large fist, awkwardly pushed the helmet aside, and muttered to himself, "Where am I going?"

It was Ralph! He had borrowed the armor from the unconscious soldier and put it on himself.

Now he had to enter the soldier's game without being discovered. It was risky, but Ralph needed that medal!

Dressed in the armor, Ralph made his way through Game Central Station. He was headed for the soldier's home game, a new game called *Hero's Duty*.

Ralph picked up the pace, which was difficult because he had trouble seeing out of his new helmet. He stumbled, then accidentally tripped over his little homeless friend, who was walking forlornly through the station.

Ralph raised his visor and looked down.

"Oh, sorry, there," Ralph said. The orange character looked at Ralph curiously.

Moving on, Ralph noticed that people were saluting him. Some were even waving, and nobody backed away. Ralph scratched his head and continued walking.

He strode all the way to the entrance to *Hero's Duty* without anyone giving him a hard time.

Then he saw Surge Protector. Ralph sighed and waited for the usual grilling.

"Name?" Surge Protector asked. Then he looked at Ralph's uniform and saluted. "Oh, sorry, soldier. Proceed."

Ralph saluted back. Then he proudly walked into *Hero's Duty,* thinking, *So this is what it feels like to be a Good Guy.*

CHAPTER

7

At Litwak's Family Fun Center, Mr. Litwak opened the arcade for the day. A crowd of kids rushed to get inside.

It wasn't long before quarters were dropped into *Hero's Duty,* the new, big-screen, first-person-shooter game. A little gap-toothed girl with red hair picked up her game pointer, ready for action. She stared at the screen and listened anxiously as the booming voice of the game's narrator said, "On a planet with no name, a top-secret experiment has gone horribly wrong."

At the same time, the game characters were lining up, getting ready inside a troop transport ship. Ralph and a few other soldiers arrived just in time.

"Quarter alert! Quarter alert!" a voice called out. Ralph followed the soldiers as they rushed toward their starting positions.

"Hustle up!" a soldier named Corporal Kohut yelled

out. "Game time." Ralph continued with the other soldiers into the hull of a dark ship. Kohut looked over to Ralph.

"Feeling better, Markowski?" he asked.

"What?" Ralph replied, startled. Then he realized—*he* was Markowski! Ralph grinned. "Oh! Yeah, I'm good," he said. "In fact, I'm so good, I'm ready to win a medal."

Just then, the soldiers stepped aside as the first-person shooter, a little robot moving on wobbly mechanical wheels, rolled in. Its flat-screen head displayed the face of the little gap-toothed girl. This little robot would be her eyes and ears during the game, and at the console, she would control its movements.

The narrator's voice blared: "Game play in three, two, one."

"We are humanity's last hope," snarled Sergeant Calhoun, leader of the platoon. She was tall, fit, and tougher than nails. She continued, explaining everything to the player. "Our mission: destroy all cy-bugs."

The doors of the ship's hull opened.

Ralph found himself looking out into a bleak, twisted, metallic landscape. Giant scorpionlike bugs swarmed around a tall, futuristic building that jutted into the sky. Ralph was pushed out of the ship with the other soldiers.

"Ahhhhh! No! What have I done?" Ralph shouted as he fell onto the terrain. Huge quivering cy-bugs seemed to be everywhere—in the air, on the ground, and heading toward the platoon. "Help me!"

As the bugs swarmed in, Calhoun didn't bat an eye. She pointed to the building in the background.

"There it is," she said. "Ninety-nine levels of mayhem, and the Medal of Heroes for the bravest who makes it to the top."

She looked over her shoulder. A giant black bug was flying directly at them. "Cy-bug. Twelve o'clock!" she said coolly.

Ralph looked up, saw the most grotesque insect he'd ever seen, and screamed. "Oh, this was a horrible idea!" he howled, dashing out of the bug's way.

Ralph fled through the chaos. He realized in horror that cy-bug eggs were all around him. The eggs hatched quickly, growing into ferocious adults as he watched. And whenever they ate something, they transformed into a crazy version of their meal. When one cy-bug ate a jeep, it turned into a bug with wheels. Another swallowed a gun, and one of its claws grew into a weapon.

"When did video games become so violent and scary?" Ralph shrieked.

Calhoun shot a cy-bug that was about to eat Ralph. Then she grabbed him and threw him aside. "Markowski! Get back in formation before I rip your head off!" She turned to the first-person shooter and shouted, "The entrance to the lab is right across that bridge!"

Ralph made a run for it, thinking he'd find some safety in the building. But as he did, the lab doors flew open and an even larger swarm of cy-bugs poured out.

"AH!" Ralph yelled, reversing position as the bugs came at him. "Save me! Save me! Take her!" Ralph howled as he fled, holding the first-person shooter up in front of him like a shield.

Seconds later, the booming voice called out, "Game over!" Ralph kept running, and then turned to see whether the bugs had taken the bait. They had completely covered the first-person shooter!

CHAPTER

8

The game's narrator called out, "Game reset. Game reset." A bright beacon of light shone up through the top of the building and into the sky.

"BEACON UP!" Kohut yelled. "Cease fire!"

Immediately, the cy-bugs stopped fighting and turned toward the light. Clouds of bugs flew toward the beacon. Each one was zapped into oblivion with a sizzle as it touched the light.

"Return to start positions," the game announcer said.

Calhoun abruptly turned her attention to Ralph. "Markowski!" she yelled.

"Sir. Yes, sir!" Ralph shouted. Calhoun hit him square on the head.

"What's the first rule of *Hero's Duty*?" she asked, her face no more than an inch from Ralph's nose.

"No cuts, no buts, no coconuts?" Ralph replied.

She hit him again and yelled, "Never interfere with the first-person shooter! We're already facing the most dangerous enemy in this arcade. We don't need you making the experience more interesting. So stick with the program, soldier! Do you hear me?"

Ralph nodded, and Calhoun walked away. "Back to start positions," she commanded.

"Yeah, right," Ralph whispered to himself. "I'm not going through *that* again." He looked up at the ninety-nine levels of the building. "The medal's up at the top," he said, thinking there must be an easier way.

Meanwhile, in the real world, the little gap-toothed girl who had been playing the game made a beeline from *Hero's Duty* to another game called *Sugar Rush*.

She stared at the game's opening screen, which featured a selection of nine colorful racers and candylike letters that read RANDOM ROSTER. NEW RACERS DAILY. She smiled. "Sweet!" She started to put her quarter on the machine to reserve the next game, but two bigger kids nudged her out of the way.

"Go away, kid," they told her. "We're playing all nine of today's racers." The little girl sighed and moved away.

She took her quarter over to *Fix-It Felix Jr.* instead. It was an older game with simple graphics, but it was still fun. A happy musical introduction played as 8-bit video trucks built the Niceland apartment building. Then Nicelander characters moved into their apartments.

A quote bubble popped up at one side of the screen: "I'M GONNA WRECK IT!" But the balloon's pointer led to no one. Wreck-It Ralph didn't appear.

The little girl pushed a button, but nothing happened. "Huh? Where's the wrecking guy?" she asked, confused.

Inside the game, the Nicelanders were asking the same thing. "Where's Ralph? He should be wrecking the building," Roy whispered.

"Shhh. Stick with the program," Gene replied.

After a pause, the Nicelanders all shouted, "FIX IT, FELIX!"

Felix jumped onto the screen holding his magic hammer. "I CAN FIX IT!" he declared. Then he looked at the building—there was no Ralph and nothing to fix. Through a gritted smile, Felix whispered, "Ralph. Quarter alert. Game on."

Using the joystick, the little girl made Felix bounce in front of the building. The Nicelanders were completely flustered. "What do we do?" Gene asked.

"Just act naturally," Felix replied. "I can fix it." Ignoring what the little girl's joystick indicated, he climbed down the building and ran to Ralph's garbage pile, out of sight of the game's screen. "Ralph! Ralph! Ralph!" he yelled. But Ralph was nowhere to be found.

In the arcade, the little girl was very confused. She'd never seen Felix behave like that before. "Mr. Litwak!" she yelled.

Old Mr. Litwak scurried right over. "What's the trouble, sweetheart?"

"The game's busted," she complained.

Mr. Litwak took a look at the *Fix-It Felix Jr.* screen.

"Whoa, boy!" he said, and gave the machine a good kick.

Inside the game, the building rumbled and the Nicelanders began screaming. Mr. Litwak shook his head and placed an OUT OF ORDER sign on the screen.

The Nicelanders could see the arcade lights dim as the sign covered their console window. They read the words backward in shock.

"Ladies and gentlemen," Gene announced, "we're out of order."

"Ralph has doomed us all!" Lucy cried.

"I don't want to be here when the plug is pulled," Roy

41

whimpered. All the Nicelanders began to panic.

"Now, everybody calm down," Felix said. He tried to reassure them that Ralph was probably just late returning from Game Central Station, when he noticed a light coming toward them through the power cord. "See, there he is now!" he said.

But when the train arrived, it wasn't carrying Ralph.

It was Ralph's homeless friend.

"What brings you here, neighbor?" Felix asked.

The orange character blurted out a stream of information in his own language, which sounded like nonsense to most of the Nicelanders.

"What's he saying, Felix?" Gene asked anxiously.

Felix did understand the gibberish, and his jaw dropped in shock. "Ralph went to *Hero's Duty*!"

CHAPTER

9

Inside *Hero's Duty*, Ralph was climbing up the outside of the lab building. "Ninety-seven . . . ninety-eight . . . ninety-nine," he huffed, until he finally reached the top.

Peering through a window, Ralph could see the Medal of Heroes hanging in the center of the room, at the top of a short set of stairs. Ralph smashed the window and climbed in.

On the ground below, Calhoun led her soldiers back toward their starting positions. The game's narrator intoned, "The arcade is now closed." That meant the soldiers could relax just a little. No more kids would play the game until the next day.

Suddenly, Calhoun sniffed the air and snapped, "Quiet. Someone's coming."

A transport from Game Central Station pulled up, and Calhoun saw someone step off it. Someone who definitely didn't belong in her rough-and-tumble game.

Felix, looking small and vulnerable, peered around. Calhoun immediately tackled him.

"What are you doing here?" she barked.

"I'm Fix-It Felix Jr., ma'am," he said, "from the game *Fix-It Felix Jr.*" Then he looked closer at Calhoun and gasped. "Look at that high definition in your face!"

Calhoun tried to hide a glimmer of a smile before she shouted, "Now state your business!"

Felix stood up and took off his hat respectfully. "I'm looking for my colleague, Wreck-It Ralph."

Calhoun did not believe Felix, and was telling him to return to his own game when they both heard a loud noise. Everyone turned to look at the lab building. There was Ralph's giant body silhouetted against a window on the ninety-ninth floor.

Ralph didn't know or care that he was being watched. He was focused on his task as he cautiously headed toward the medal. Thousands of cy-bug eggs were packed into the room, so he had to tiptoe around them, picking his way toward the medal.

Finally, with a sigh of relief, he walked to the center of

the room. Then, like a dream, the glistening Medal of Heroes swept down out of the light and settled around his neck. Heroic music filled the room, and the images of generals saluted him. The game narrator announced, "Congratulations, soldier! You are the universe's greatest hero."

Ralph stood tall and puffed out his chest proudly. He couldn't help thinking of all the wonderful things that were going to happen to him now that he had a medal.

But as Ralph shifted his stance, one of his feet hit an egg.

"Oopsie," he said as the egg tipped over and smashed open. A baby cy-bug tumbled out. It looked up at Ralph. Then it jumped onto his face.

"AH!" Ralph yelled, stumbling backward. Unable to see, he tripped and fell into a seat at the edge of the room. A harness immediately locked him in place. The seat swiveled around, pushing him into a small spaceship. The spaceship's door slammed shut.

"Escape pod activated," a voice announced. The engines fired and—*BOOM!* With the cy-bug still clinging to his face, Ralph's ship launched from the top of the building.

Ralph kicked and flailed, trying to pull the cy-bug off his face. His feet hit buttons on the dash, and the ship careened all over the sky. With a *whoosh,* it headed toward the soldiers.

"Incoming!" Kohut shouted.

The ship twirled and dipped and zoomed across the sky, right past Calhoun and Felix. Both of them gasped—they could clearly see through the pod's front window.

"Ralph!" exclaimed Felix.

"Cy-bug!" snarled Calhoun.

CHAPTER
10

Inside Game Central Station, Ralph's pod blasted through the terminal, spiraling like a bottle rocket off the floor and walls. Ralph punched his face, trying to force the disgusting bug away. Finally, he tugged it off.

"Ha-ha!" Ralph cried triumphantly. But then the bug started growing fast.

With no one to steer it, the escape pod whirled down the first tunnel it hit, leaving Game Central Station and barreling along a dark power cord. The blackness inside the cord slowly turned bright pink. Globs of pink goo slapped onto the pod's windshield and got sucked into the engines, making a horrible grinding noise.

"Engine failure," the ship's robotic voice announced as the ship nosed downward violently.

"AH!" Ralph yelled, and the force of the downward plunge lifted him out of his seat. Then the pod crashed.

Ralph and the cy-bug, now huge, slammed against the dashboard. Just then, something beeped. Ralph and the cy-bug turned to look. It was the *eject* warning alarm.

In an instant, they were both launched into a strange new world. Ralph landed on top of a peppermint tree. The cy-bug bounced off the tree and sank into a pool of green taffy.

Ralph sighed in relief to see the end of the bug. Then he looked around at the sugarcoated world he'd landed in.

A starter pistol went off in the distance, and Ralph could hear a cheering crowd. From his perch high in the tree, he looked over a nearby cliff and saw a candy racetrack and a bunch of go-karts whizzing by. "Where the heck have I landed?" he asked himself. Then he saw a giant sign spelled out with candy: SUGAR RUSH.

"Sugar Rush?" Ralph moaned. "Oh, man, this is that candy go-kart game!" He rolled his eyes. "I gotta get out of here!"

Then he glanced downward . . . and realized that his medal was no longer around his neck. "Huh? Oh, no-no-NO! My medal!" he wailed. But something golden was glimmering high up in another peppermint tree.

The medal! It must have flown off when he was ejected

from the ship. Quickly, Ralph dropped down through the branches.

He stepped across a bubbling taffy pool, grabbed the trunk of the tree, and began to climb.

Ralph was making steady progress upward when a voice above him said, "Hi, mister."

CHAPTER

11

"Aahh!" Ralph yelled. Looking into the tree branches, he could see a little girl with a crooked smile. She was looking down from the branch above him, and she was wearing a green hoodie. Her hair was tied up with a long strip of red, rubbery licorice.

Ralph sputtered, "You scared me, kid! What are you doing—sneaking up on people?"

"What's your name?" the girl asked.

"Wreck-It Ralph," Ralph replied.

"You're not from here, are you?" she said, noticing there was nothing candylike—or even very sweet—about Ralph.

"No, well . . . yeah, I mean, not from right in this area. But I'm doing some work here," he said.

"What kind of work?" the little girl asked.

Ralph kept climbing. "Some routine candy trimming,"

he said. "You probably want to stand back. In fact, this whole area is technically closed while we're trimming, so—"

"Who's 'we'?" she asked.

"Uh, the candy tree department," Ralph replied.

"Are you a hobo?" she asked impishly.

Ralph was beginning to get annoyed. "No, I'm not a hobo. But I am busy. So go on, now. Go home."

"What's that?" she said. "I didn't hear you. Your breath is so bad, it made my ears numb."

"Okay. That's rude," Ralph grumbled, and kept climbing higher. "And this conversation is over."

"Uh, I wouldn't grab that branch if I were you," the girl said.

Ralph rolled his eyes and grabbed the branch anyway. "Look, I'm from the candy tree department, so I know exactly what I'm—" *DING!* A bell sounded. And *SNAP!* The branch broke. Ralph fell and just barely managed to grab a lower branch with one hand.

"Double-stripes break," the girl explained with a grin, referring to the candy cane design that covered the branch. "Ga-DOY. Hey, how come your hands are freakishly big?"

"Uh, I don't know," Ralph replied. "How come you're so freakishly annoying?"

The girl looked up and noticed the glistening medal. She gasped. "Sweet mother of monkey milk! A gold coin!"

"Don't even think about it. That is mine!" Ralph yelled.

"Race you for it!" she challenged, swinging quickly up through the peppermint branches.

Ralph followed her. He grabbed a double-stripe and—*DING!*—he felt the branch break under his hand.

"Double-stripe!" the girl called as she grabbed the medal from the treetop. "The winner!"

Ralph reached up to the branch where she was standing and flung her off. She dropped the medal, and Ralph caught it in his huge hand. Then—*DING!* Ralph landed on a double-stripe and fell. The medal went flying.

"Double-stripe!" the little girl shouted.

"Aahhh! Noooooo!" Ralph said as the girl snagged his medal. He was hanging just inches above the taffy swamp.

"Thank you," she said to Ralph.

"Wait, let me just talk to you for one second. Here's the thing. I'm not from the candy tree department."

The girl frowned and shook her head. "Lying to a child?" she scolded. "Shame on you, Ralph."

"But I wasn't lying about the medal," Ralph said. "It's mine. It's precious to me. That thing is my ticket to a better life."

The girl hopped off the tree and jumped over the bubbling taffy. "Yeah, well, now it's *my* ticket," she said. Suddenly, her image began to flicker. Parts of the little girl blinked on and off, briefly. She was *glitching*! It happened sometimes in video games: when a game's code was flawed, it could cause flickering images called glitches.

"See ya, chump," the girl called out to Ralph as she took off.

"Come back! I'll find you! I will find you!" Ralph said, reaching for a branch. He heard a *DING!* and looked up.

"Double-stripe!" the little girl yelled as Ralph tumbled into the gooey swamp. He popped up, looking like an enormous taffy beast before slipping down again into the sticky stuff.

CHAPTER

12

Inside Game Central Station, Surge Protector was showing Calhoun, Kohut, and Felix the damaged entrance to *Sugar Rush*. By now, everyone knew that Ralph had caused the destruction.

"Yeah," Surge Protector said, pointing to the battered tunnel. "He banged off the walls something awful, and then he flew right down there like some sort of hotshot."

"*Sugar Rush*, huh?" Calhoun said.

"So what now?" Felix asked.

Calhoun looked at Felix as if he were crazy. "What are you, thick? There was a cy-bug on that shuttle!" When he didn't respond, she continued, "Do you even know what a cy-bug *is*?"

"I can't say that I do, ma'am," Felix replied.

"Cy-bugs are like a virus. They don't know they're in a game. All they know is eat, kill, multiply. Without a beacon to stop them, they'll consume *Sugar Rush*." She let that sink in, and then added, "And once those cy-bugs finish off *Sugar Rush*, they'll invade every game in this arcade!"

As she walked away, Felix turned to Kohut. "Is she always this intense?"

"It's not her fault," Kohut replied, looking serious. "She's programmed with the most tragic backstory ever. The one day she didn't do a perimeter check was her wedding day."

Calhoun stared down the dark tunnel and returned to the awful memory that haunted her. She and Brad were facing each other, about to recite their wedding vows, when a giant cy-bug crashed through a stained-glass window above them. To everyone's horror, its jaws grabbed her handsome groom. Calhoun fought and defeated the evil bug, but nothing could bring back her beloved.

Calhoun shook off the memory as Felix cautiously approached her. "Ma'am, I'm going with you."

"Negatory," she replied.

"It is my job to fix what Ralph wrecks," Felix insisted, standing his ground. "No flex on this one, ma'am. I am coming along with you."

Calhoun nodded, and then whipped out her cruiser, which looked like a surfboard hovering over the ground. Felix hopped on the back, and the two headed into the power cord that led to *Sugar Rush*.

Each night when the arcade closed, the racers from *Sugar Rush* came out and competed against each other to see who would be included in the Random Roster list for the following day's game. Everyone in the game liked to watch, and tonight, the stands were full. The racers zipped up to the starting line in their cake and candy go-karts as the crowd cheered. The announcer, Sour Bill, called out, "Introducing the Rightful Ruler of *Sugar Rush,* King Candy!"

King Candy rose from his throne and grabbed the microphone. "Hello, my loyal subjects! Ha, ha! Have some candy!" he shouted, throwing handfuls of sweets into the crowd.

Beneath the stands, the little girl with Ralph's medal was pushing a small vehicle covered with a tarp. She peeked out from the shadows, holding the medal clenched between her teeth.

"And now for our main event!" King Candy declared in

a loud voice. "The Random Roster Race!"

The little girl tucked the medal in her pocket, pulled up her hood, and put on some sunglasses.

"Just in time," she whispered to herself.

King Candy continued addressing the crowd. "As you all know, this is a qualifying race. The first nine contestants to cross the finish line will represent *Sugar Rush* up there as tomorrow's avatars." He pointed to the CHOOSE YOUR RACER screen.

"Race! Race! Race!" the crowd cheered.

"Yes. Okay. Calm down!" King Candy raised his hand. "Listen, this event is pay-to-play. The fee to compete is one gold coin from your previous winnings, if you've ever won, which—ha, ha, ha!—I have. Let me go first."

King Candy held up his gold coin and threw it into the air. It was caught in a colorful candy rainbow slide and swept into a giant pot above the racetrack. King Candy's name appeared on the contestants' board by the starting line. The crowd went wild!

The next racer, a strawberry-pink go-getter named Taffyta Muttonfudge, tossed her coin up. Her name lit up on the roster, and the crowd cheered again. One after another, the names of the racers filled the board: Rancis Fluggerbutter, Adorabeezle Winterpop, Minty Zaki,

Jubileena Bing-Bing, and all the rest.

The little girl knew this was her chance. Stepping out from the shadows, she gave Ralph's medal a kiss for good luck and tossed it into the air. The coin was caught by the candy rainbow, and then it rolled around the rim of the pot before finally dropping in. The pot glitched briefly, and the girl held her breath.

King Candy covered the microphone and leaned over to Sour Bill. "Who's that last one?" he asked, nodding toward the hooded figure below.

The board glitched for a second, and the last racer's name appeared in lights: VANELLOPE VON SCHWEETZ!

"Vanellope?" King Candy exclaimed.

Vanellope raised her arms in victory. "I'm in the race!" she cried, flickering slightly.

"It's the glitch!" someone in the crowd yelled. Taffyta Muttonfudge ripped the tarp off Vanellope's little vehicle, revealing a pile of recycled junk, shaped into a go-kart. LICKETY-SPLIT was written on the sides.

The crowd began to panic, rumbling and shouting.

"It's all right," King Candy told them. "Don't be alarmed! Security! Security!"

The Donut Police, Wyntchell and Duncan, came running in.

"Come here, kid," Duncan called to Vanellope. She looked at the two cops and made a break for it.

"How did she get a gold coin?" King Candy asked Sour Bill.

"Must have stolen it," Sour Bill muttered grumpily.

And just at that exact moment, Ralph barreled onto the tracks, yelling, "Give me back my medal, you little thief!" He was coated in taffy, peppermint twigs, and bits of candy. He looked like a huge, crazy candy monster.

Wyntchell took one look at him and panicked. "RUN!" he squealed.

The crowd watched in shock as Ralph chased them all down the track, screaming, "MY MEDAL!"

CHAPTER
13

King Candy was beside himself with worry. "Heavens to unleavened bread! What is that?" he asked as Ralph tore through the stadium, destroying go-karts and breaking the rainbow slide.

Ralph shook off a kart that was stuck to his foot, launching it toward the spectators. The crowd scattered.

Vanellope slipped under a spectators' box, but Ralph reached in and dragged her out.

"Let go, Franken-stench!" Vanellope yelled as she squirmed and threw candy in Ralph's face.

"AH! RED HOTS! My eye!" Ralph howled.

Vanellope wiggled out of Ralph's grip. "See ya, chump," she said, and scurried back under the stands.

"Now you're gonna get it!" Ralph said, following her. The stands rose up and splintered as Ralph's huge body lumbered underneath.

"Ah!" King Candy cried out in despair. "We just had those shellacked!"

As Vanellope zipped out from under the broken stands, Ralph tried to follow. But he knocked over a tower, which launched a big cupcake into the air. It tumbled and fell right onto him. His head popped out of the top, and his feet came out the bottom. He could only waddle.

"Give me back my medal!" he cried as he watched Vanellope escape.

Then, to completely ruin Ralph's day, Wyntchell and Duncan rushed in and began hitting him with their batons.

"Hey! What're you doing?" Ralph yelled.

King Candy's voice came over the loudspeaker. "Okay, folks. Calm down! The monster's been caught. We'll repair all the damage. Don't worry! We will have our race before the arcade opens!"

Vanellope looked up at the racers' board and grinned. "And I'm in it!" she said proudly.

King Candy looked up at the board. "Sour Bill, that glitch cannot be allowed to race." Then he pointed to Ralph in the cupcake. "And bring that *thing* to my castle."

Outside King Candy's castle, cookie guards marched in formation. The Donut Police rolled Ralph, still covered in taffy, into the throne room. He was encased in the giant cupcake and completely immobilized. He remained helpless as King Candy drove in on his go-kart and backed it into his throne, which was also a parking spot.

"Sour Bill, de-taffify this monster so we can see what we're up against here," King Candy said.

Sour Bill pulled a giant glob of taffy off Ralph's face.

King Candy gasped. "Wreck-It Ralph? What are you doing in my game?"

"Long boring story," Ralph replied. "Now, if you could just give me back my medal—"

King Candy seemed surprised. "Your medal? You mean the coin the glitch used to buy her way into our race?"

"Bingo!" Ralph said.

"But you're the Bad Guy," King Candy said. "Bad Guys don't win medals."

"Well, this one did. I earned it over in *Hero's Duty.*"

"You game-jumped?" King Candy asked. "You're not *going Turbo,* are you, Ralph?"

"I just want my medal back!"

"Tough taffy," King Candy said. "Once it's in the pot, it's just code—and it stays that way until someone wins."

"I'm not leaving without my medal."

King Candy nodded. "Yes, you are. Wyntchell, Duncan, get him out of that cupcake and on the first train back home." King Candy revved his go-kart. "Now I've got a glitch to deal with, thanks to you. So goodbye, Wreck-It Ralph. It *hasn't* been a pleasure!" he called, and drove off.

The two donuts came over and rapped on Ralph's cupcake. "That thing's hard," said Duncan. "Get the tools!"

When Ralph realized the police were getting out a chain saw, he decided not to stay and see what happened next. He waddled down the hallway and dived out the window.

CHAPTER

14

When Ralph hit the ground, the cupcake split apart, and Ralph was free. He jumped to his feet and ran.

Without knowing where he was going, Ralph raced through Lollistix Forest until he finally ran out of steam. He could hear the Donut Police coming after him with a pack of pastry bloodhounds—the cake dogs were yapping wildly, not far behind. Still panting, Ralph started up again, this time disappearing into a ravine.

The cake dogs stopped when they came to a chocolate stream. They sniffed around, but they'd lost Ralph's scent. They turned back.

They didn't notice a candy straw poking straight up out of the stream. The straw slowly moved toward the shore. Then Ralph lifted his head up from the stream and spit out the straw, which had been helping him breathe.

"I hate chocolate," he muttered.

When it comes to battling cy-bugs, Sergeant Calhoun is the best of the best.

Ralph heads toward the glowing beacon at the top of the laboratory—but so do the cy-bugs!

Ralph finds more trouble than he expected when he winds up in the *Sugar Rush* video game.

King Candy is the ruler of *Sugar Rush*. He loves to race, but most of all, he loves to win.

Vanellope von Schweetz wants to enter
the *Sugar Rush* Random Roster Race.

It's time for the race to begin!
The racers line up in their candy go-karts.

Vanellope thinks Ralph is a stink brain, and he thinks
she's annoying, but they make a great team!

Suddenly, Ralph heard the clanking sound of metal tools hitting the ground. He peeked over a hill and saw Vanellope adjusting the pedals of her rickety kart. Spare parts littered the ground all around her.

Angry, Ralph started down the hill after her. Then he stopped. A stream of racers was zooming down the road.

"There she is!" Taffyta Muttonfudge yelled. The racers skidded to a stop in front of Vanellope. Vanellope looked at them, glitching a little.

"Hello, fellow racers," Vanellope said in a friendly tone. Her image flickered in and out of focus, glitching a bit, as she greeted them. "Come to check out the competition?" she asked. "Well, here it is: the Lickety-Split, the ultimate driving machine."

Taffyta and the racers circled around Vanellope.

"Vanellope, you have to back out of the race," Taffyta said, frowning.

"Oh no, I don't," Vanellope replied, a little surprised. "I paid my fee, and I'm on the board. So I am definitely racing."

"But you know the rules," Taffyta told her. Rancis handed Taffyta a scroll. She opened it and began to read: "'By royal decree: glitches may never, ever, ever race.'" She unrolled the scroll some more and showed a circle-slashed picture of Vanellope at the bottom.

"I'm not a glitch," Vanellope said. "I've just got pixlexia, okay?"

"Pixlexia?" Taffyta asked skeptically.

"Uh, a code-reading disability," Vanellope said, hoping they'd believe it. "It occurs when the corpus does not properly recognize certain symbols."

From up on the hill, Ralph thought to himself, *Huh, good to know.* Then he heard Vanellope tell Taffyta, "I'm definitely racing."

"No," Taffyta said haughtily. "You're not a racer. You're a glitch, and that's all you'll ever be." Taffyta began to shake, imitating Vanellope's glitch. A couple of other racers joined in and started laughing. Then they turned to Vanellope's kart.

Ralph was shocked. "Uncool," he said to himself. "Just uncool."

Then the bullies began smashing Vanellope's kart. "I want that spoiler," Rancis said, ripping a piece off the kart.

"I'll take the fenders," another racer said.

"Stop it! Wait!" Vanellope shouted, running to protect her kart. "You're breaking it!"

One of the racers pushed her down, and Vanellope

landed in a mud puddle with a splat. Ralph gritted his teeth and clenched his huge fists. He knew exactly how it felt to be pushed into the mud.

"Leave her alone!" he shouted. He ran down the hill, flailing his huge arms.

"Ah!" Taffyta screamed. The racers were terrified to see Ralph coming at them. They jumped into their karts and zoomed off.

Ralph turned to Vanellope. He watched her wipe away tears as she sifted through the wreckage of her go-kart.

"What are *you* looking at?" she said, sniffling.

"You're welcome, you rotten little thief," Ralph grumbled, even though he really did feel sorry for the kid.

"I'm not a thief. I just borrowed your stupid coin. I was going to give it back to you as soon as I won the race. Besides, it's just one stinking medal," Vanellope told him. "Go back to your game and win another one."

"I can't," Ralph mumbled. "Guys like me don't win medals in my game."

Vanellope looked up. "Well, where'd you get it, then?"

"In *Hero's Duty,*" Ralph replied.

"*Hero's Doodie?*" Vanellope snorted as she made a weak attempt to stifle a giggle. "I bet you really gotta watch where you step in a game called *Hero's Doodie.* Ha, ha!"

"How dare you insult *Hero's Duty*!" Ralph said indignantly. "I *earned* that medal, and you better get it back for me!"

Ralph raised his fists in frustration and began to wreck some rock candy that was nearby. Vanellope watched him break up the landscape, then she turned back to her kart and sighed.

"This is hopeless," she muttered. She took another look at Ralph, who was wrecking everything in the background. "Unless . . . ," she whispered to herself.

"Uh, feeling better now?" Vanellope asked Ralph in her sweetest voice.

"Not really," Ralph replied. "What's it to you?"

"Well," Vanellope continued, "while you were throwing a tantrum, I think I figured out how to get your medal. Here's what I'm thinking: you help me get a kart, a real kart, and I'll win the race and get you back your medal."

Ralph stared at her in disgust. "You want me to help *you*?"

Vanellope shrugged. "All you gotta do is break something for me. C'mon, what do you say, friend?" She held out her tiny hand.

"We are not friends," Ralph replied.

Vanellope smiled and looked at him hopefully. "Come

on, buddy. Let's shake on it. Aw, come on, chumbo. Ralph, my man. My main man. Hey, my arm's getting tired. We got a deal or not?"

Ralph shuffled his big feet and reluctantly shook her hand. "You better win," he warned.

CHAPTER
15

Felix rode behind Calhoun on her cruiser as the two followed Ralph's path of destruction into *Sugar Rush*'s Candy Cane Forest. Calhoun shook her head at the sight of all the smashed peppermint trees. "Well, I'll say this much: they don't call your friend Wreck-It for nothing."

Calhoun spotted Ralph's crashed shuttle and checked the cockpit. "Is he in there?" Felix asked.

"Nope. Lucky for him. Otherwise I would have slapped his corpse," Calhoun said, frowning. "No cy-bug, either."

Turning back to the trees, Calhoun took out her bug detector and scanned the area. "Got to find that bug before it lays its filthy eggs." The device showed a faint signal, which disappeared a moment later. "This atmosphere is full of sugar particles. They're jamming up my sensor."

With a sigh, she turned to Felix. "So, what's going on with Wreck-It?" she asked. "What's his agenda?"

"I wish I knew, ma'am," Felix said. "He was acting all squirrelly last night, going on about cake and medals. But I never thought he'd do something like this. I never thought he'd go Turbo."

"What do you mean, 'go Turbo'?" Calhoun asked.

"Well, back when the arcade first opened, *Turbo Time* was by far the most popular game in the arcade. And Turbo loved the attention. Maybe a little too much."

Felix thought back, remembering what the video game character Turbo looked like—a big smiley face on a pixilated red-and-white car. When Turbo won a race, he would stand on the awards podium and exclaim, "TURBO-TASTIC!"

"But then a new racing game came along and stole his thunder," Felix continued. He remembered the day they'd wheeled the new game into the arcade. All the kids had abandoned Turbo in mid game to play the new console.

"Boy, was Turbo jealous—so much that he did the unthinkable! He abandoned his game and tried to take over the new one." As kids played the new game, the 8-bit Turbo drove all over the racetrack and caused the players to crash their cars. It wasn't long before the kids were yelling for Mr. Litwak.

"Turbo ended up putting both games—and himself—

out of order, for good." Felix sighed. "I can't let that happen to my game."

"Don't worry," Calhoun said, her voice softening a little. "We'll find Wreck-It."

BREEP! The bug sensor suddenly went off, and Calhoun jumped to her feet. "This way!" she yelled.

Felix followed, hurrying through the bushes after her.

The two jumped through an opening in the underbrush and landed in a hollow filled with chocolate powder. They were covered up to their waists. Some vines hung down from above them, but no matter how they stretched, the vines were too far away.

Calhoun was the first to realize what was happening. "It's quicksand!" she cried. "Don't fight it! The more we fight, the faster we'll sink."

Calhoun huffed angrily. "I've survived a thousand cy-bug battles, and now I'm going to die in a pile of chocolate-powder milk mix."

Felix couldn't help giggling. Calhoun glared at him. "I just got it!" he explained, pointing to a small sign next to the pit. It read DANGER: NESTLÉ QUIK-SAND! He laughed even louder.

As he did, the vines above the pit began to rustle. Then they stretched and grew down toward the chocolate powder. "It's Laffy Taffy!" Felix gasped. He turned to Calhoun. "You've got to laugh! Laugh as if your life depends on it!"

"I don't laugh," she snarled.

Felix knew how to fix that. "Here comes the tickle monster," he said teasingly, his fingers reaching out to tickle Calhoun's arm.

It took a little while, but soon Calhoun was giggling. To get back at Felix, she tickled him, too. Before long, they were both laughing uncontrollably.

The Laffy Taffy vines rustled and grew faster. Finally, they reached down to Felix and Calhoun. The two grabbed on and were lifted to safety, still giggling.

"What is this feeling?" Felix asked, smiling dreamily.

Calhoun grinned. "I haven't laughed this hard since . . ." Her voice trailed off.

Felix looked at her expectantly. Hopefully.

"Brad." Calhoun's expression became hard, and her eyes narrowed. "Time to look for more bugs," she told Felix. "Better fix that shuttle—we'll get a better read from the air. Can you fix it?"

"Yes, I can fix it," answered Felix sadly.

Together they started walking back toward the wrecked escape pod.

CHAPTER
16

Vanellope led Ralph through *Sugar Rush* to a building that was shaped and decorated like a huge birthday cake. They sneaked past a security booth with a guard snoozing inside.

Reaching the building, they found a huge deadbolted door blocking their way. A picture of Vanellope was painted on the door, with a red slash through it. Underneath, it read NO GLITCHES ALLOWED!

"Here it is, knuckles," Vanellope whispered. "Do your thing. Break it."

"You want me to break in?" Ralph said.

"You want me to have the best kart, don't you?" Vanellope asked.

Despite its size, the door was no match for Ralph's fist. In no time, he and Vanellope were inside. The interior was huge—a cross between an auto factory and a giant bakery kitchen. It was a special bakery for candy go-karts!

"Where's the kart?" Ralph asked.

"We've got to make it," she said.

But that was easier said than done. The first step was to flip through the recipe box, a giant box full of huge cards.

Vanellope quickly found a recipe she liked. The picture on the card showed the coolest, slickest kart she had ever seen.

"All right, let's get to work!" she said.

"No, no," Ralph protested. "Listen, kid, I don't make things, I break things . . . for a living. I'll ruin it."

Vanellope didn't care. She started right in, preheating the oversized oven and dragging ingredients toward the gigantic mixing bowl.

She couldn't carry the huge bag of flour because she was so small. "Look out, grease monkey," Ralph said finally. He threw the bag over his shoulder. As he dumped it into the bowl, a white cloud puffed up and covered them both with white flour.

After that, they worked together quickly. When Vanellope had trouble stirring the batter, Ralph pushed her aside. "Stand back," he told her. "I'm gonna mix it." Then Ralph did what he did best: he pounded the batter with his giant fists.

The batter splashed everywhere, but Vanellope cheered, "Yes, yes!"

After the oven timer dinged, Ralph pulled the kart mold out of the oven and released the kart's chassis. Vanellope immediately shoved a cookie tire onto one axle, while Ralph pushed a hard candy tire onto another. Then she wrapped a licorice fan belt around the engine, and Ralph poured maple syrup into the fuel container.

By the time they got to the frosting, Ralph realized he was having fun. Then he squeezed his pastry bag too hard and hit Vanellope in the face with purple frosting. She just laughed and squeezed green frosting right back at him! Soon sprinkles, gumdrops, and candies were flying everywhere.

The sound of laughter and the aroma of baking wafted through the air and out the building. The guard suddenly woke with a start. He looked at the security camera and saw Vanellope!

Grabbing his red emergency phone, he shouted, "The glitch is in the garage!"

CHAPTER
17

Inside the garage, Vanellope's newly baked racing kart was finally ready, emerging from a cloud of powdered sugar.

Although he'd had fun, Ralph knew the new kart looked nothing like the picture on the recipe card. He gazed at the pathetically lumpy, crazy-looking kart and sighed. "Kid, I hate to say I told you so, but I tried to warn you. I don't build. I wreck."

Vanellope stood silently, staring at the kart with wide eyes. Then she clasped her little hands and said, "It's perfect!"

"It is?" Ralph asked.

"I love it! I LOVE IT!" Vanellope cried, running over to kiss the kart. She picked up a pastry bag, the cone-shaped kind that bakers use to create icing swirls, and handed another one to Ralph. She motioned for him to sign his name.

"Come on!" she declared excitedly. "A work of art like this must be signed."

Carefully but proudly, Ralph wrote MADE BY RALPH. Vanellope signed her name, too.

Vanellope and Ralph stepped back and admired their work.

"Look at you," Vanellope said, "all proud of what you made."

Suddenly, a familiar voice yelled out from the other side of the garage. "I've got you now, glitch!" It was King Candy, furious. "And Wreck-It Ralph? Why is *he* still here?"

"Oh, boy. Time to go," Ralph said, throwing Vanellope into the driver's seat of the kart.

Vanellope began to glitch anxiously as she revved the engine . . . but the car didn't move. Finally, she looked up at Ralph. "Um, I don't know how to drive a real kart," she said.

"You don't *what*?" Ralph yelled. He grabbed Vanellope and put her on his shoulders. He hopped into the driver's seat and used his giant arms and hands to propel them along. Moving as fast as he could, Ralph aimed them at the garage window.

"You lied!" Ralph shouted as they busted out into the

open. "You promised you'd win the race, and you can't even drive?"

King Candy and the Donut Police were hot on their trail as Ralph pushed the kart quickly along the road. "Stop in the name of the king!" yelled King Candy.

"Get off the road!" Vanellope shouted to Ralph. "Head for Diet Cola Mountain!"

At a fork in the road, Ralph headed toward the tall mountain towering above the landscape. "Now drive into the wall!" Vanellope cried.

"What?" Ralph gasped.

"Right there. In between those lollipop sticks!"

"Are you crazy?" Ralph screamed.

"Just do it!" Vanellope shouted.

Ralph aimed the car at the side of Diet Cola Mountain and braced for the impact.

CHAPTER

18

King Candy heard Ralph scream as they hit the wall of the mountain and disappeared. The king and his Donut Police screeched to a halt, but they couldn't see where Ralph and Vanellope had gone.

"Find that glitch!" King Candy yelled as he hopelessly scanned the landscape. "She can't be allowed to race!"

Meanwhile, to Ralph's surprise, he, Vanellope, and the kart burst through the wall and skidded to a stop. They were completely unharmed, and the wall showed no sign of a crash.

Ralph looked around at the inside of the mountain. It was a large open area littered with rocks, as well as debris from the game. A dark lake filled the middle of the cavern, and a huge white stalactite hung down over the center, suspended from a high ceiling. He could see a nearby sign that read DIET COLA HOT

SPRINGS—BEWARE OF FALLING MENTOS!

"Where am I?" Ralph asked.

Vanellope gestured all around her and said, "Welcome to my home!"

Ralph stared at the stalactite, which was made of round, white mints. As he did, a small chunk of candy broke off and dropped into the diet cola. A chemical reaction immediately caused a small glowing geyser to spurt into the air. "Watch out for the splash," Vanellope advised. "That stuff's boiling hot!"

Then she smiled. "I found that secret opening over there and claimed this place as my own. Pretty cool, huh?" She motioned to a pile of candy wrappers. "See, I sleep here. I like to bundle myself up like a little homeless lady. It's fun."

Ralph was appalled. "No," he said, thinking this was even worse than his dump. "This isn't fun, because you're supposed to win back my medal, and you don't know how to drive."

"Well, no, not technically," Vanellope admitted. "I just thought—"

"What did you think?" Ralph said in a mocking tone. "'Oh, yes, I'll just magically win the race because I really want to.'"

"Listen, wise guy, I know I'm a racer!" Vanellope replied, her eyes narrowing. "I can feel it in my code."

"That's it. I'm never getting my medal back." Ralph threw his hands up in resignation.

"What is the big whoop about that crummy medal, anyway?" Vanellope asked.

Ralph sighed. "Well, this may come as a surprise to you, but in my game, I'm the Bad Guy."

Vanellope rolled her eyes.

"Yes, and nobody likes me, and I live in garbage."

"Like candy wrappers?" Vanellope asked. Perhaps she and Ralph were more alike than she'd originally thought.

"Worse," Ralph replied sadly. "Bricks."

"Yeah, well, at least you belong in your game. Everyone here says I'm a mistake and I shouldn't even exist."

"If nobody wants you, why don't you just leave?" Ralph asked.

Vanellope looked at him and shook her head. "See, glitches can't leave their games. It's one of the joys of being me." She sighed.

Ralph shrugged. "Well, there are no joys to being me. But that medal is going to change all that."

"Really? How?" Vanellope asked.

Ralph stared off dreamily. "It proves I'm someone

who matters, and when I get home I'm going to live in a penthouse and get pies and go to parties with ice sculptures, and I'll be on top of the cake. It's a lot of grown-up stuff; you wouldn't understand."

"No, I get it," Vanellope said. "That's exactly what racing would do for me."

Then Ralph got an idea. He stood and started to break up some of the rocks around Diet Cola Hot Springs.

"Hey! What are you doing?" Vanellope cried. "Come on! I know it's a dump, but it's all I've got!"

Ralph continued to smash rocks and debris all around the lake. If he couldn't fix something, he would break enough stuff to *make* something. "If you're going to win that race, then you need to learn to drive," he said. "And you can't do that without a track, can you?"

"Wow!" Vanellope said, watching as Ralph placed her kart on his newly created practice racetrack.

"Okay," Ralph said, pointing to the kart. "Now, this is the steering wheel."

"Ga-doy," Vanellope said, rolling her eyes.

"Don't be a wise guy," Ralph told her.

Still, that was as far as Ralph could take the lesson. He saw pedals and levers. But he had no idea what to do with them, because he didn't know how to drive, either.

Vanellope was eager to experiment, though. The first time she hit the gas pedal, the go-kart took off like a rocket and slammed into a rock. She spit something out of her mouth. "It's okay," she shouted, "just a tooth!" Then she took off again.

In time, the kart stopped stalling every few seconds and began to zip steadily around the track. Vanellope whooped happily.

"Whoa. That's good," Ralph called out. "Look at you! You're doing it. You're awesome! Now bring 'er in."

But Vanellope kept going. "I'm going off-road!" she yelled, zooming toward a broken ramp. Ralph covered his eyes as Vanellope went airborne, glitched crazily, and then landed safely on the opposite side.

Then she glitched some more . . . all while zipping past the minty stalactite, shaking shards of it into the Diet Cola Hot Springs. Ralph jumped out of the way as giant geysers shot into the air. She careened off the stalactite, caught some twisted track, and screeched to a halt at his feet.

"So, how'd I do?" she asked, grinning.

"Are you crazy?!" Ralph gasped. "If that stalactite fell, it would blow up this whole mountain! You've got to get that glitching under control!"

"I will, I will," Vanellope told him with a grin. "Just tell me, you think I got a chance?"

"Tiny," Ralph replied. Then he smiled at her and said, "Top-shelf."

Vanellope raised her scrawny arms in victory. "Yes! Yes! I'm gonna win!" She jumped up and fist-bumped Ralph before getting back in the seat and taking off again.

CHAPTER
19

Meanwhile, down in the lowest levels of the castle, King Candy approached a heavy door with a large combination lock. He glanced back to make sure no one was watching, and then pulled out a sheet of paper. The title at the top read CHEAT CODES.

The king set to work on the lock, looking at the codes and entering the required sequences. Finally, the door clicked and swung open.

Inside was no ordinary room—it was a dark area, stretching off into what seemed like infinity. Tethering himself to a cord, King Candy kicked off into the dark space and swam toward a floating structure not far away. Delicate and complicated, it appeared to be made up of hundreds, maybe thousands, of small rectangular bricks, suspended together in a delicate orb of glowing threads. He looked at the orb in awe as he reached its outer edge.

"The code," King Candy murmured to himself. "The sweet lifeblood of this game!"

As he floated through the center of the web, King Candy reached out and sorted through various digital images passing by.

"Hmm. Let me see. . . . Aha! There you are!" The king spotted a digital image of coins from the Random Roster Race, including the Medal of Heroes! He grabbed Ralph's medal and yanked it out. As he did, the medal glitched from digital code back into its original solid form. He nodded with satisfaction.

The king quickly swam back toward the door opening and stepped into the castle. He shut the door and locked it tight. The medal was tucked safely in his pocket.

"I'm going out!" he shouted to Sour Bill as he ran toward his kart. "You're in charge of the castle until I get back!"

At that moment, Calhoun and Felix were aboard the shuttle, flying over *Sugar Rush,* scanning the terrain for any trace of cy-bugs. Felix, his cheeks still aglow, stared longingly at Calhoun.

"Sergeant Calhoun?" Felix said nervously. "I was just

wondering. Maybe one evening after work we could meet up and share a root beer float . . . with two straws?"

Calhoun looked sharply at Felix, noting his red cheeks and puppy-dog eyes.

Suddenly, she banked the ship hard to the right. Without saying a word, she brought the shuttle to the ground, landing in Lollistix Forest. King Candy's castle was visible just over the rise.

"All right, this is where we part ways," she said to Felix.

"What?" he asked. "Was I being too forward? You can have your own root beer with your own straw."

Calhoun's eyes narrowed. "I've got a cy-bug to hunt down. I'm sure the pixie sticks living in that castle can help you find your friend. Now good-bye."

She bumped Felix out of the shuttle and slammed the door shut.

Still confused about what had just happened, Felix looked around. He walked in a daze to King Candy's castle and knocked on the door.

"Mmmm . . . yes?" Sour Bill said as he opened the door.

"Hi. I'm Fix-It Felix Jr. Have you seen my friend Ralph?"

"You mean Wreck-It Ralph?" Sour Bill asked.

"Yes. That's him. I've been so worried."

Sour Bill eyed Felix suspiciously. "We should have

locked him up when we had the chance," he said, reaching for a lever inside the doorway. "I'm not making the same mistake with you." He pulled the lever, and a trapdoor opened under Felix's feet. Sour Bill smiled as he watched Felix drop into the darkness.

CHAPTER
20

Inside Vanellope's mountain, Vanellope and Ralph were pushing her go-kart out the secret entrance. As they headed down the road, Vanellope was smiling, but she was flickering like crazy.

"Hey, hey, calm down," Ralph said. "You're glitching like a deranged hummingbird."

But Vanellope was too excited to calm down. "Am I ready to be a real racer?" she asked. "What if the players don't like me?"

"Who doesn't love a brat with dirty hair?" Ralph scoffed. "Come on! The players are gonna love you."

Vanellope laughed and jumped into her kart. Ralph climbed on the back.

"Now, if you get nervous," he said, "just keep telling yourself, 'I must win Ralph's medal or his life will be ruined.' And have fun! Got it?"

"Got it," Vanellope said as she began to drive. Then she slammed on the brakes. "Wait! Hold on! I forgot something. Be right back."

Ralph shrugged as Vanellope ran back into the mountain.

A low-riding candy car flew around the bend. It screeched to a halt, and King Candy stepped out.

"You!" Ralph yelled.

"No, no! I come alone, unarmed." King Candy held out his empty hands.

"I've had enough of you!" Ralph yelled, lunging at the little man. He picked King Candy up by the lapels and demanded, "What do you want?"

"I just want to talk to you," King Candy replied, looking terrified.

Ralph refused to put him down. "I'm not interested in anything you have to say."

"Well, how about this?" King Candy said, pulling the Medal of Heroes from his pocket. "Are you interested in this?"

Ralph dropped the king. "How did you get it?" he asked.

"It's yours!" King Candy waved his hand generously.

Ralph stared at the precious medal and sighed.

"All I ask," King Candy said, "is that you hear me out."

"About what?"

"Ralph, do you know what is hardest about being a king? Doing the right thing." King Candy paused. "I need your help. As sad as it is, Vanellope cannot be allowed to race."

"Why are you people so against her?" Ralph blurted out.

"I'm not against her. I'm trying to protect her. If Vanellope wins that race, she'll be added to the roster." King Candy went on to explain that she would begin to glitch. She would be seen on the screen, and everyone in the arcade would assume something was wrong with the game. The game would be unplugged and put out of order—forever!

"All my subjects will be homeless," King Candy finished, "but there is one who cannot escape, because she's a glitch."

Ralph realized that King Candy was talking about Vanellope.

"When the game's plug is pulled, she'll die with it," King Candy finished.

Ralph imagined the OUT OF ORDER sign being placed on *Sugar Rush* and the characters escaping to Game

Central Station—except little Vanellope. She would be sucked into the vortex of unplugged oblivion.

Ralph shook his head. "You don't know that'll happen," he whispered. "The players could love her."

"Are you willing to bet her life on it?" King Candy asked. As he spoke, he dangled the medal in front of Ralph's face. "Now, it says here that you're a hero. I don't think a hero would let her get in that kart, Ralph."

"Promise me you'll stop hassling her," Ralph demanded. But his voice was wavering.

"As the Rightful Ruler of *Sugar Rush*, I swear I won't lay a finger on her," King Candy declared. He smiled sadly as he handed the medal to Ralph. Then he returned to his kart and drove away.

Ralph took the medal reluctantly. He looked at the go-kart he and Vanellope had built together. When he saw Vanellope come out of the mountain, he sighed and put the medal in his pocket. He knew what he had to do.

CHAPTER

21

Vanellope was fired up and ready to race. "I'm back," she said excitedly. "Did you miss me?"

"Oh. Yeah," Ralph replied. "Hey, can we talk for a second?"

"Wait," Vanellope said. "First, kneel down."

"What? No, no, no," Ralph answered.

"Just do it!" Vanellope said. Ralph dropped to his knees. "Now close your eyes."

"Vanellope," Ralph objected.

"Shush. Close 'em," she said as she tied something around his neck. "Okay. Open 'em!"

Ralph looked down and saw a homemade medal hanging from a string. It read TO STINK BRAIN.

"Turn it over!" Vanellope ordered anxiously.

Ralph saw YOU'RE MY HERO painted on the back.

"I made it for you, in case we don't win," she said. Ralph

felt awful. "Now rise, my royal chump!" she continued. "I've got a date with destiny!"

Ralph didn't budge. "Um, I've been thinking—"

Vanellope laughed. "That's dangerous."

"Vanellope, you can't be a racer," he said finally.

"Ha-ha. That's not very funny, Ralph."

"I'm not joking. I'm gonna be straight with you, kid. I was talking to King Candy, and—"

"King Candy!" Vanellope cried. Then she noticed the *Hero's Duty* medal hanging out of his pocket. Her eyes widened. "Wait a minute. You sold me out?"

"Listen. You don't understand," Ralph pleaded.

"No, I understand plenty, traitor," she said. "You're a rat! And I don't need you! I can win the race on my own!"

Vanellope jumped into her go-kart and started to take off. But Ralph grabbed the kart's rear bumper. "Let me go!" Vanellope shouted. Ralph took Vanellope out of the kart and hung her by her hood on a pointy gumdrop.

"No. I'm doing this for your own good," he said. Then he raised his huge fist and smashed the go-kart to pieces.

"Stop! No! Ralph! No!" Vanellope shrieked, bursting into tears. "You really *are* a bad guy!"

Ralph picked up his *Hero's Duty* medal and walked down the road alone.

Soon Ralph was riding on the train back to *Fix-It Felix Jr.* The Medal of Heroes was around his neck. As the train pulled to a stop, he looked up at the Niceland apartments. The building was dark, except for a single light at the top.

Ralph went up to investigate. He pushed himself through the door and found Gene alone. Gene looked at the medal around Ralph's neck.

"Well, I'll be!" Gene murmured. "You actually went and did it. You took my challenge to heart and won a medal. Of course, you destroyed our game in the process."

"Huh?" Ralph replied, confused. "Where is everybody?"

"They're gone, Ralph. After Felix went to find you and then didn't come back, everyone panicked and abandoned ship."

"But I'm here now," Ralph said.

Gene shook his head. "It's over, Ralph. They're pulling our plug in the morning." He pointed to the OUT OF ORDER sign. "But never let it be said that I'm not a man of my word. The place is yours, Ralph. Enjoy."

"Gene, wait, this is not what I wanted," Ralph pleaded.

"I was just . . . tired of living alone in the garbage."

Gene shook his head. "Well, now you can live alone in the penthouse."

After Gene left, Ralph stood in the silent penthouse. Then he walked out onto the balcony. He felt even worse now than before. Getting a medal had seemed like a simple solution, a straightforward way to earn respect and friendship. Instead, not only had he lost Vanellope as a friend, he'd also ruined his entire game.

Frowning, Ralph ripped the Medal of Heroes off his neck. He threw it at the OUT OF ORDER sign on the game screen.

The screen shook a little and the sign slipped slightly, just enough to let Ralph look out into the empty arcade . . . and he saw the *Sugar Rush* game across the room.

Suddenly, he noticed something: a picture of Vanellope on the side of the *Sugar Rush* console!

Ralph's jaw dropped. So Vanellope *wasn't* just a glitch. She *belonged* in the game!

Ralph raced from the Nicelanders' building and dashed toward *Sugar Rush*.

CHAPTER

22

Ralph ran straight to Diet Cola Mountain, where he'd last seen Vanellope. Sour Bill was there, picking up the pieces of Vanellope's broken kart. Ralph loomed over him with his huge hands on his hips.

"Would you mind explaining something to me, cough drop?" Ralph asked. "If Vanellope was never meant to exist, why is her picture on the game console?" Sour Bill froze.

"C'mon. Talk!" Ralph barked. "What's going on?"

"Nothing," Sour Bill insisted.

Ralph put his face next to Sour Bill's hard-candy body. "I will lick you," he growled.

"You wouldn't," Sour Bill said, trembling.

Ralph gave him a quick lick.

"I'll take it to my grave!" Sour Bill howled.

"Fine," Ralph replied, and tossed Sour Bill into his

mouth. Sour Bill let out a muffled scream, and Ralph pulled him out.

"Okay, I'll talk! I'll talk!" Sour Bill cried. "She was supposed to be in the game, and King Candy tried to delete her, but he could never find all of her code."

"He *made* her a glitch?" Ralph asked angrily.

Sour Bill nodded. "He'll do anything to keep her from crossing the finish line and becoming a real racer."

"Why?" Ralph asked.

"I don't know. I mean, I literally cannot remember. Nobody can," Sour Bill replied, shaking his head.

"Where is she now?" Ralph asked.

"In the dungeon with Fix-It Felix. And that's all I know, I swear. Please don't put me in your filthy mouth again." Ralph gave him a lick and stuck him to a tree. Then he scooped up the remains of Vanellope's kart and took off.

In a licorice field, Calhoun was staring at her scanner. She followed its beeping cautiously. The signal faded in and out as she moved forward. "Ugh," she said. "Saccharine-saturated nightmare."

Suddenly, the sensor's signal went off, loudly! Calhoun looked around in confusion. "But where . . . ?" That's when the ground beneath her gave way . . . and she fell into a giant underground cavern.

Clinging to a web of licorice roots, Calhoun could see that the space below her was full of cy-bug eggs. A few little bugs had already hatched and were skittering across the ground. She gasped as she grappled with the roots, trying not to fall. "Doomsday and Armageddon just had a baby and it is ugly," she said grimly, her eyes sweeping over the cy-bugs' nest.

Things were suddenly looking much, much worse.

Inside his cell, Felix alternately paced and banged frantically on the iron door. The arcade would be opening in less than an hour. "Hello! Somebody? Anybody! Please let me out! I need to get home!"

He noticed a loose bar in his cell's window. "I can wreck it," he said, and banged on it with his hammer. But the bar only got stronger. "Oh, why do I fix everything I touch?" Felix moaned.

Just then, Ralph burst through the wall.

"Felix!" he shouted, dumping the broken pieces of Vanellope's kart at his feet.

Felix threw his arms around Ralph.

"Oh, Ralph! I'm so glad to see you. Wait—no, I'm not. What do you have to say for yourself?" Felix said, looking at the mangled parts at his feet. "What is that?"

"It's a go-kart," Ralph replied. "I wrecked it. You have to fix it."

"I don't have to do *boo*!" Felix told him. "Do you have any idea what you've put me through? I ran higgledy-piggledy all over creation looking for you. I almost drowned in chocolate milk mix. And I met the most dynamite gal. She gives me the honey glow something awful! But she rebuffed my affections. And then I got thrown in jail. You've no idea what it's like to be rejected and treated like a criminal!"

"Yes, I do," Ralph replied. "That's every day of my life. That's why I ran off and tried to be a Good Guy." He motioned to the go-kart parts. "But there's a little girl who really needs our help, right now. You fix her kart here and I promise, I will never try to be Good ever again," he said.

"Oh, Ralph," Felix said, touched by Ralph's selfless desire to help someone else. He reached for his golden hammer and got to work.

Elsewhere in the dungeon, Vanellope sat sadly in her own cell. King Candy had placed her in a room with no bars or windows. And to be sure she couldn't escape, he had fastened chains around her waist and ankles.

There Vanellope sat, unable to move, when—*BAM!*—her cell door crashed open and in rolled Ralph in her beautiful, completely fixed go-kart. Ralph jumped forward and broke Vanellope's chains.

"I know, I know," he told her. "I'm an idiot."

Vanellope looked at him sternly, raising an eyebrow. "And . . . ?" she asked.

"And a real numbskull," Ralph said.

"And . . . ?" she asked again.

"And a selfish diaper baby."

"Annnnnd . . . ?"

"And a stink brain?"

Vanellope beamed. "The stinkiest brain ever!" she exclaimed happily. At last, they were a team again!

CHAPTER

23

At the *Sugar Rush* race arena, a giant soda bottle display was shooting out fountains of orange, cherry, and grape soda. The red-and-white popcorn boxes were filled with screaming fans, and the racers were at the starting line.

The Donut Police guarded the exits as King Candy stood in his royal box. He was feeling quite pleased. The little glitch was nowhere in sight.

"My sweet subjects!" he declared. "I can assure you that I have never been so happy in all my life to say the following words: let the Random Roster Race commence!"

The crowd cheered as King Candy slid down a royal banner and landed in the seat of his go-kart, ready to join the race. A floating marshmallow waved a checkered flag, and the racers zoomed off the starting line.

Taffyta and Rancis came out strong. King Candy hit a button and a cannon appeared on the hood of his kart.

It fired red globs of frosting, which caused some of the racers to spin out. King Candy quickly jumped from fifth to first place.

The racers sped down the track, and the crowd followed all the action live on a jumbo video screen.

Finally, Vanellope raced up to the starting line, with Ralph and Felix holding on for dear life. "Remember," Ralph told her as he and Felix jumped off. "You don't have to win. Just cross that finish line and you'll be a real racer."

"I'm already a real racer," Vanellope replied. "And I'm going to win!"

The crowd screamed in horror as Vanellope sped onto the track. But she didn't care—in no time, she was zipping through Gumball Alley, dodging the giant gumballs, and catching up to the other racers.

"Oh no! It's the glitch!" Rancis shouted.

As the pack zoomed up a mountainous chocolate cake, Taffyta shouted to one of the other racers: "Light 'em up, Candlehead!"

With a burning candle on her helmet, Candlehead leaned over and lit the stems of all the cherries decorating the cake as she raced up the incline.

But these were no ordinary cherries—they were cherry

bombs! One by one, the bombs exploded, barely missing Vanellope.

Concentrating hard, Vanellope stayed right behind the pack as the group soared off the top of the cake and into a giant straw.

"Stay sweet, glitch!" Taffyta called, as sprinkle spikes shot out the back of her kart.

Surprised by the attack, Vanellope began glitching all over the place, totally out of control inside the straw. Suddenly, she glitched right between the other racers— and ended up in front!

In shock, the other racers lost control and went flying off the track. The crowd gasped as they all spun out, crash-landing in a series of giant red velvet cupcakes. They were out of the race.

Down in the stadium, Ralph and Felix were cheering as they watched Vanellope move up to second place on the contestant board.

"Let's finish this thing without any more surprises," Ralph shouted happily.

At that moment, Calhoun arrived—and punched Ralph in the face. "Hope you're happy, Johnny Disaster-seed," she said. "This game is going down, and it's all your fault."

"My lady?" cried Felix. "You came back."

Felix's joy turned to worry as Calhoun quickly explained that the escaped cy-bug had not perished in the taffy swamp, as Ralph had thought. Instead, it had multiplied. Now everyone was in danger.

Before she could even finish her warning, the ground began to shake and crack open. Huge cy-bugs burst out!

CHAPTER

24

On the track, Vanellope caught up with King Candy on the double helix portion of the course. He took the blue spiral track and she took the pink.

"Hello!" Vanellope shouted.

King Candy was stunned. "Vanellope? How did you break out?"

Vanellope smiled. "I didn't break out, I wrecked out!" she said, and cut him off, taking the lead.

Back at the stadium, Calhoun fought off the bugs as she helped the crowd out of the stands. "We must evacuate to Game Central Station immediately. Hurry!"

Ralph could see the cy-bugs swarming over the finish line, attracted to the glow of the signs. He ran over and started punching them. "Shoo! Go back to your own game!" he yelled. He knew that Vanellope still needed to cross the finish line or she would stay a glitch. And as a glitch, she would never be able to leave the game.

As Ralph, Calhoun, and Felix fought, the Random Roster Race was still visible on the jumbo screen. Vanellope was heading into Nougat Mine, with King Candy right on her fender.

"Get off this track!" King Candy yelled, as his kart rear-ended hers. "I forbid you to cross that finish line!" He broke the antenna off his kart and began whacking her with it, to make her lose control of her kart.

Both Ralph and Felix looked up at the screen, worried to see Vanellope in danger.

"I'm not letting you undo all my hard work!" King Candy shouted at Vanellope.

Glitching, Vanellope reached over, trying to protect herself, and pushed the king away. But as her hand touched his face, King Candy began to glitch, too! He glitched in strange flashes of red and white . . . transforming into an oddly familiar face.

"Is that . . . ?" Felix asked in shock.

Ralph couldn't believe what he was seeing. "No! It can't be!" he gasped at the sight of the pixilated smiley face.

"TURBO!" they both said. At the same time, a wave of recognition swept through the crowd.

"Turbo!" they all shouted in a panic.

As Vanellope's hand pulled away, Turbo's appearance glitched back into the form of King Candy. But his secret was out. "You've ruined everything!" he yelled at Vanellope. Swerving, he tried to ram her into a wall. "End of the line, glitch!"

Vanellope could see the wall coming at her, and it looked like she would be forced to crash. But hearing King Candy yelling, she had an idea. Concentrating very hard, she repeated to herself, "Glitch, glitch, GLITCH!"

And then she *did* glitch—at exactly the right time to move aside and miss the wall. King Candy was very surprised, especially because her move made *him* smash into the wall instead! His kart skidded, flipped, and spun out.

Vanellope flew past him, heading for the finish line. "Woohoo! I did it!" she yelled happily.

"Bring it home, kid!" Ralph shouted. "Finish line's wide open!"

But as Vanellope drew close to the end, cy-bugs were everywhere. Vanellope screamed as she crashed into a bug that burst out of the ground in front of her. The bug turned, ready to attack.

Ralph ran to Vanellope and scooped her up. The arena was full of bugs now, and the finish line was collapsing.

"Oh no," Felix said, as the finish line disappeared entirely. "I can't fix that."

While Ralph and Felix wondered what to do, King Candy emerged from the racetrack tunnel and veered toward the finish line. The destruction caught the king by surprise, and he was furious. "Cy-bugs! No, no! Where did they . . . ?" He paused, realizing how all this had happened. "Game jumper!" he screamed at Ralph. "You wrecked my beautiful game. I'll get you, Ralph! I'll get you if it's the last thing I—"

His shrieking was cut short as a cy-bug flew down and grabbed him in its pincers. *CHOMP!*

King Candy had become a cy-bug meal.

CHAPTER

25

"Everybody out, now!" Calhoun shouted. She stood at the top of the rainbow bridge leading to Game Central Station, directing everyone toward the exit tunnel.

All around, swarms of vicious cy-bugs filled the air. *Sugar Rush* would not last much longer.

Finally, Ralph and Vanellope came running up the rainbow bridge, among the last to arrive.

Then Vanellope stopped.

"Ralph," she said, "I told you, I can't leave the game."

"We gotta try," Ralph said as he hoisted her on his shoulders and tried to push through the exit. But Vanellope kept hitting an invisible wall.

"It's no use," she said, looking up at him.

"No!" Ralph said softly, placing his giant hands gently on Vanellope's little shoulders. He looked into her eyes. "I'm not leaving you here alone."

"Everyone's out," Calhoun shouted. "Now we've got to blow up this exit!"

Calhoun knew that if she couldn't contain the cy-bugs, they'd spill into Game Central Station. From there, they would destroy every game in the arcade.

"I'm so sorry, kid," Ralph said to Vanellope.

"It's okay," Vanellope said.

But Felix was still upset. "What about this game?" he asked Calhoun.

"There's nothing we can do," she replied. "Without a beacon, there's no way to stop these monsters."

"Beacon?" Ralph exclaimed. He remembered how the cy-bugs had swarmed to the light in *Hero's Duty,* and that gave him an idea. He looked across *Sugar Rush* and stared at the top of Diet Cola Mountain.

"Stay with Felix," Ralph told Vanellope.

Then he turned to Felix. "As soon as the bugs are dead, fix that finish line and get her across it."

Felix tried to stop his friend. But Ralph moved quickly, stepping onto Calhoun's cruiser and speeding off toward Diet Cola Mountain.

"Ralph, no! Wait!" Felix hollered. "What are you doing?"

Ralph didn't answer. He was on his way to do the only thing he could to save Vanellope.

CHAPTER

26

Ralph nearly fell off the cruiser as he punched the flying cy-bugs out of his way. When he finally landed at the top of Diet Cola Mountain, he jumped off the cruiser into the mountain's crater. Its center was minty white. Ralph knew that the huge Mentos stalactite hung just below the surface. If he could get the Mentos to fall into the Diet Cola Hot Springs, they would blow the top of the mountain off with a glowing geyser of boiling white light. The volcano would create the beacon that Calhoun needed to get rid of the cy-bugs!

Ralph punched the center of the crater. Bits of the stalactite dropped down into the pool below. He just had to punch a little more. Then—

Whoosh! Ralph was lifted into the air. It was King Candy! Sort of. His body was half cy-bug now, with candy pincers and wings. Part of his face looked like King

Candy, and part looked like Turbo.

"Uh-oh," Ralph said.

"Have some candy, Ralph," the King Candy-bug snarled.

The creature glowered at Ralph, yanking him by the leg. "Up we go!"

As he was dragged into the sky, Ralph could see Vanellope far below. The bugs were closing in on her. Then he looked down at the volcano, swiftly growing smaller in the distance. Desperately, he wondered if he still had any chance of starting the beacon.

At that moment, the King Candy-bug flipped Ralph around in the air and caught him by the back of his shirt. The creature raised a sharp pincer and pointed it at Ralph. "Game over, Bad Guy!" the bug said, about to strike.

But Ralph twisted, suddenly breaking free from the bug's grasp. He fell toward the ground.

As he fell, Ralph grasped the little heart-shaped medal Vanellope had given him. He read the words on it: YOU'RE MY HERO. Ralph knew he was doomed, but he also knew he would do anything to save Vanellope.

"I'm Bad and that's good," Ralph recited to himself. "I will never be Good and that's not bad. There's no one I'd rather be than me."

And with that, Ralph slammed through the candy

crater at the top of the mountain. Below him, the giant minty stalactite cracked and then plunged, taking Ralph with it. He knew that when the mint hit the cola, there would be a boiling-hot volcanic eruption!

Ralph closed his eyes and braced himself for the end.

Suddenly, at the last possible second, Ralph heard the roar of a go-kart. Vanellope was zooming around the track inside the mountain. She expertly glitched and steered her go-kart just the right way to catch the falling Ralph.

Together they rocketed away from the stalactite, just as it splashed into the cola and—

KA-BOOM!

The two friends were blown into the air by the blast. They landed in a pool of chocolate—sticky, but safe.

As the eruption's beacon of glowing light filled the sky, the cy-bugs' tails began to hum and wag. Every bug stopped what it was doing and began flying toward the volcano. As the bugs flew into the hot diet cola, they immediately vaporized with a sizzling *ZAP!*

ZAP!

ZAP!

ZAP!

ZAP!

From down below, Ralph and Vanellope stared in awe.

Then even King Candy's cy-bug body began to rise toward the glowing lava fountain.

The Turbo-king part of the creature flailed its arms, unable to subdue its bug instincts. Desperately, the evil racer reached out and grabbed the branch of a peppermint tree. It halted him . . . momentarily. Then—*DING!*

"Oh no—double-stripe!" the King Candy-bug moaned as the branch broke. His cy-bug body flew into the glowing beacon. *ZZZZZZAP!*

The selfish reign of Turbo was finally over.

CHAPTER
27

Ralph and Vanellope dragged themselves out of the chocolate and exchanged a grin. "I love chocolate!" Ralph told her.

With all the cy-bugs gone, everyone gathered back at the finish line. Felix went straight to work, fixing it with his hammer. In no time, the twisted track was pieced back together.

Ralph lifted Vanellope and her kart onto the track.

"You ready for this?" he asked.

"Ready as I'll ever be," Vanellope said. Ralph gave her a push, and watched as Vanellope rolled across the finish line.

Inside the dark room where King Candy had kept the game's code, lines of broken code repaired themselves. The entire *Sugar Rush* game glitched, and then the landscape was reset to its original dazzling beauty. The rainbow that led to *Sugar Rush*'s power cord entrance re-formed. *Sugar Rush* was back to normal!

Out on the track, Vanellope rose magically from her kart in a cloud of sparkling pink sugar.

"Whoa. What's with the magic sparkles?" Vanellope said as she twirled around in midair.

A beautiful princess dress formed around Vanellope's little body, and a crown appeared on her head. She drifted down next to Ralph.

Sour Bill declared, "Hail to the Rightful Ruler of *Sugar Rush:* Princess Vanellope!"

As the game repaired itself, everyone realized that Vanellope was indeed *Sugar Rush*'s real ruler. When Turbo had changed the game's programming, it had affected their memories. But now that the game had been repaired, they were no longer confused.

All the racers ran up to Vanellope. "We're so sorry about the way we treated you," Taffyta said.

"Can you ever forgive us?" Rancis asked.

Vanellope smiled. "Tut-tut. As your merciful princess, I hereby decree that anyone who was ever mean to me shall be . . . immediately executed!"

The racers began to wail and cry.

"Yes. Heads cut off. Chop, chop," Vanellope said,

grinning. The racers' wails grew louder. "No. I'm just kidding. Stop crying."

"I'm trying. It won't stop," Taffyta bawled.

Ralph turned to Vanellope. "So this is the real you, a princess?" he asked.

"No, *this* is the real me," Vanellope replied, throwing her crown aside. Instantly, she glitched back into her old self, green hoodie and all.

"Look," she said, "the code may say I'm a princess, but I know who I really am—a racer with the greatest super power ever!"

"Super power?" asked Ralph.

"Yeah," Vanellope replied happily. "Did you not see me on the racetrack? I was here. I was there. I was driving through walls. Glitching is my super power. I'm not giving that up."

"But without a princess, who will lead us?" Wyntchell asked.

"*Me,*" Vanellope replied. "I just don't want anything to do with that princess baloney. I'm thinking more along the lines of a constitutional democracy." She shoved her hands into her pockets. "President Vanellope von Schweetz has a nice ring to it. Don'tcha think?"

Ralph kneeled in front of her. "Sure does, kid. But do

me one favor. Hang on to that crown, in case you ever want to leave your game."

Vanellope smiled. "I'll take that under advisement, chumbo."

Calhoun stepped up and said, "Okay, people, the arcade's about to open. We've all got to get back to our games. So let's move out!"

Calhoun and Felix headed for the spaceship, but Ralph didn't budge. He and Vanellope looked at each other. Then she ran into his arms and hugged him tight.

"You know, you could just stay here and live in the castle," she said to Ralph. "You'd have your own wing where no one would ever complain about your stench or treat you bad ever again. You could be happy."

Ralph smiled. "I'm already happy," he said, hugging her back, "because I have the coolest friend in the world."

Then he looked over at Felix, who was standing next to Calhoun. "And besides, I have a job to do, too. It may not be as fancy as being president, but it's my *duty*."

"Ha!" Vanellope giggled.

"Ralph," Felix said, "are you coming, brother?"

"See you later, President Funnyfeathers," Ralph said.

She fist-bumped him and said, "Au revoir, Admiral Underpants."

"So long, Queen Greasy."

"Ralph!" Felix called to him. It was time to leave. Ralph nodded sheepishly and climbed into the transport.

"To be continued!" Ralph shouted to Vanellope as the transport zoomed off. He gave her a final wave with his huge hand.

And Vanellope waved right back.

CHAPTER
28

It wasn't long before Mr. Litwak unlocked the doors to the arcade. As the kids entered the game center, he walked over to the *Fix-It Felix Jr.* game and reached around the back of the console to grab the power cord.

"Wait!" the little gap-toothed girl exclaimed, watching the screen.

Mr. Litwak stared at the little girl, wondering how to tell her that *Fix-It Felix Jr.* was broken. For good.

"Look, there's Ralph," she said.

Mr. Litwak's jaw dropped. It was true!

"Ralph's back!" he cried.

Ralph was wrecking the Nicelanders' apartment building, exactly as he was supposed to.

Inside the game, Ralph climbed up the building and grabbed Gene from his window. "Ready, Gene?" he whispered.

"Ready," Gene replied, and Ralph tossed him across the screen.

Meanwhile, near the tunnel entrance to Game Central, Felix stood next to Calhoun. "Ma'am, I know there's no breaking through the iron curtain surrounding your heart, but I want to thank you. You opened my eyes to feelings I've never known."

Then they heard the Nicelanders shouting, "Fix it, Felix!"

"That's me," Felix said. "Guess I'd better—" But before he could finish, Calhoun grabbed him and planted a big kiss on his lips.

"Call me," she said. Then she stumbled into her ship and flew away.

Felix, with his cheeks aglow, ran into his game yelling happily, "I CAN FIX IT!"

Mr. Litwak looked into the console.

"Hey-hey," he said, seeing Felix enter the screen. "The gang's all there. False alarm."

Days passed, and Niceland returned to normal. Of course, there were a few changes. One night, Ralph made his way through Game Central Station and over to a Bad-Anon meeting.

"So it turns out you guys were pretty much right after all. And I sit before you a changed Ralph," he told the group.

"Jolly good," Satine said.

"Fantastic share," another Bad Guy exclaimed.

"Of course, my job didn't change," Ralph told them. "But my colleagues do seem to appreciate me more for doing it."

It was true. The Nicelanders now let Ralph enjoy the penthouse along with everyone else. They even made him a cake shaped like the apartment building, with a little Ralph on top wearing a medal.

Above the cake in sugar fireworks were the words TO OUR FAVORITE BAD GUY!

Ralph nodded at the memory. "It got me thinking about those who haven't been as fortunate as me," Ralph explained. "I mean, there is a ton of great talent just sitting out there."

He recalled the game-less characters hanging around Game Central Station. "So we took a chance and added them to our game."

Ralph smiled as he thought about his little homeless orange friend hopping around with Felix, the two of them fixing the building together. "And the players love it. They say we're *retro,* whatever that means. And remember that brick pile I used to live in? Well, I used it to build homes for our new coworkers. With a little help from Felix, of course.

"But I returned the favor," Ralph told them, "by being the best man at Felix's wedding. The whole affair went off without a hitch," Ralph said with some relief. He recalled Calhoun glancing at the church windows, expecting cy-bugs to attack at any moment. In fact, all the guests had weapons cocked and ready. But there were no bugs. Calhoun's sad backstory was over.

"But by far the best part of my day is when I get thrown off the roof," Ralph told the group. "Because when the Nicelanders lift me up, I get a perfect view of *Sugar Rush.* And I get to see Vanellope racing. She's a natural!"

Ralph loved to see the other cheering racers surrounding Vanellope when she won. They all loved her—just as he knew they would.

Ralph smiled broadly. He knew he didn't need a medal to be a good guy. "Because if that little kid likes me, how bad can I be?"